ABBY HUNTSMAN
Who Will I Be?

Pictures by Joanne Lew-Vriethoff

HARPER

An Imprint of HarperCollins*Publishers*

"Who do you want to be when you grow up?" asked Isabel's teacher.

Everyone around Isabel waved their hands in the air.
They all had an answer.

"How about you, Isabel?" Ms. Livingston asked.

"I don't know," she said.

And that bothered her.

It bothered Isabel during lunch,

during music class,

and during gym.

It was still bothering her when her dad picked her up after school.

"I don't know who I want to be when I grow up," Isabel told her dad.

"Well," her dad said, "what makes you happy?"

"Last week I went to the pool with Kayla," Isabel said. "That made me happy."

"And selling cookies at the charity bake sale was fun."

Isabel thought of another thing. "We found that man's pet parrot, remember? It made me happy that we helped him."

"Maybe you want to be someone who helps people, then?" her dad suggested.

"'Helper' isn't a *job*, Dad," Isabel replied.

"Of course it is!" her dad said. "Lots of jobs are all about helping to make the world a better place."

Isabel wasn't too sure.

"Let's take the long way home," Isabel's dad said. "I want to show you some people who have jobs helping others."

"We'll start right here, at your school," Isabel's dad said.

"Who do you see?"

"I see my teacher," said Isabel. "And I see the crossing guard."

"Your teacher helps you learn, and the crossing guard helps you stay safe," said Isabel's dad.

Isabel had never thought of it that way.

"Let's see who else we can find!" said Isabel's dad.
A man in a white coat walking a dog gave Isabel a friendly wave.

"He's a veterinarian," Isabel's dad told her.

"He helps people by making their pets feel better."

"Some people help their town by joining the police force. Or they help their whole country by joining the military," Isabel's dad told her.

"They help by keeping us safe!" Isabel said.

Isabel and her dad overheard the policeman ask an older woman, "May I walk you to the library, ma'am?"

"Let's stop at the library, Isabel," said her dad.

"Hi," whispered the librarian. "Do you need help finding a book? I could also sign you up for our book club!"

"Yes! Thank you," Isabel whispered.

"Happy to help," the librarian whispered back.

"Let's go to the park, Dad!" said Isabel.

"Can you spot the helpers here?" Isabel's dad asked her.

Isabel looked around.

She saw an activist asking those passing by to sign a petition.

She saw a gardener in a city uniform. And she saw . . .

"The garbage man!" Isabel exclaimed. "He's helping by keeping our city clean and beautiful."

There really *were* helpers everywhere.

Next Isabel and her dad passed a church.

The pastor was out front.

"What's your favorite thing about your job?" Isabel asked him.

"Helping other people," he said.

"I also like volunteering at the soup kitchen next door," he added.

"Can we help with that, too?" Isabel asked.

They worked at the soup kitchen until Isabel's dad's phone buzzed.
"Want to go meet Mom at her office?" Isabel's dad asked.

On the way, a reporter was interviewing a fireman who'd rescued a kitten. "Journalists make sure we know what's happening," Isabel's dad said.

"You should take that cat to a veterinarian in case it's hurt," Isabel told the fireman. "There's one right down the street!"

Soon Isabel and her dad arrived to meet her mom. "Mom!" Isabel yelled, and ran to hug her.

Isabel's mom worked at the mayor's office . . .

. . . because Isabel's mom was the mayor!

"I'm learning all about service," Isabel said. "Do you help people?"
"I do!" her mom said. "My job is to help the people of this city
by listening to them and passing laws to make their lives better."

Isabel had a lot to think about. There were so many different ways of helping people and so many different jobs to choose from.

"I still don't know who I want to be when I grow up," she told her dad.
"But I know one thing . . ."

"I want to be a helper."

Who Will I Be?
Text and illustrations copyright © 2018 by Abby Huntsman
All rights reserved. Printed in the United States of America.
For information address HarperCollins Children's Books, a division of HarperCollins Publishers,
195 Broadway, New York, NY 10007.
www.harpercollinschildrens.com

ISBN 978-0-06-284004-2

The artist used pen and ink and added color digitally to create the illustrations for this book.
Book design by Alison Klapthor
18 19 20 21 22   PC   10 9 8 7 6 5 4 3 2 1
❖ First Edition

Dear Reader,

When I was growing up, my grandpa would often remind me of his favorite quote: "There is no exercise better for the heart than reaching down and lifting people up." The older I get, the more I realize just how true that is. Having been raised in a family that taught me the importance of service, I wondered how I might pass those values down to my own daughter when she was born. I wrote this story hoping to show not just her but children everywhere that there are so many ways in life to help and serve others. Oftentimes, people who help others are right in front of us every day, whether it's a crossing guard making sure everyone is safe, a reporter keeping communities informed, or a teacher educating the next generation of leaders. It's okay not to know what you want to do when you grow up as long as you know you want to be a good person. Being a "helper" isn't just good for the community. It fills your life with meaning and purpose. I hope *Who Will I Be?* will inspire kids to think about others before themselves and to become "helpers" in ways big and small.

Love,
Abby